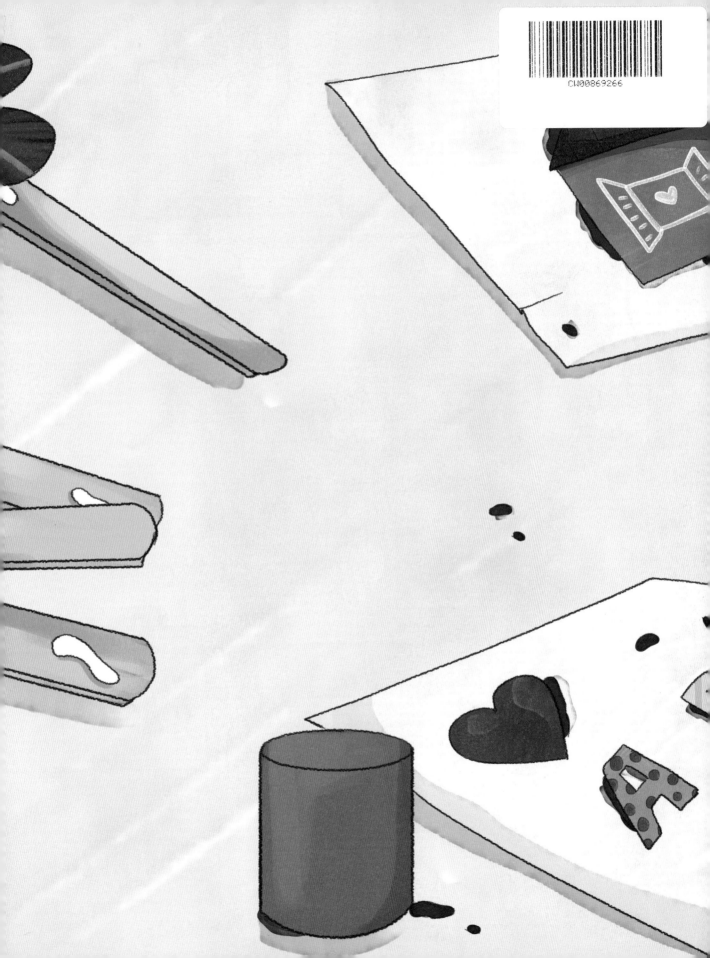

For Duane...
we're stuck like glue and I'm a little bit
braver because of you.

www.mascotbooks.com

Bottle and Stick

For more information, please contact:
Mascot Books
620 Herndon Parkway, Suite 320
Herndon, VA 20170
info@mascotbooks.com

Library of Congress Control Number: 2020920929

CPSIA Code: PRT1120A
ISBN-13: 978-1-64543-639-3

Printed in the United States

Bottle
and
Stick

Jennifer Stephens

Illustrated by Vanessa Alexandre

This is Bottle.

This is Stick.

Bottle and Stick love to help kids finish projects.

Bottle is especially good at the tough jobs. Yarn. Craft sticks. Wiggle eyes.

Stick is the kind of guy who keeps it simple. He works with all the paper. Construction paper. Scrapbook paper. Copy paper. You get the idea.

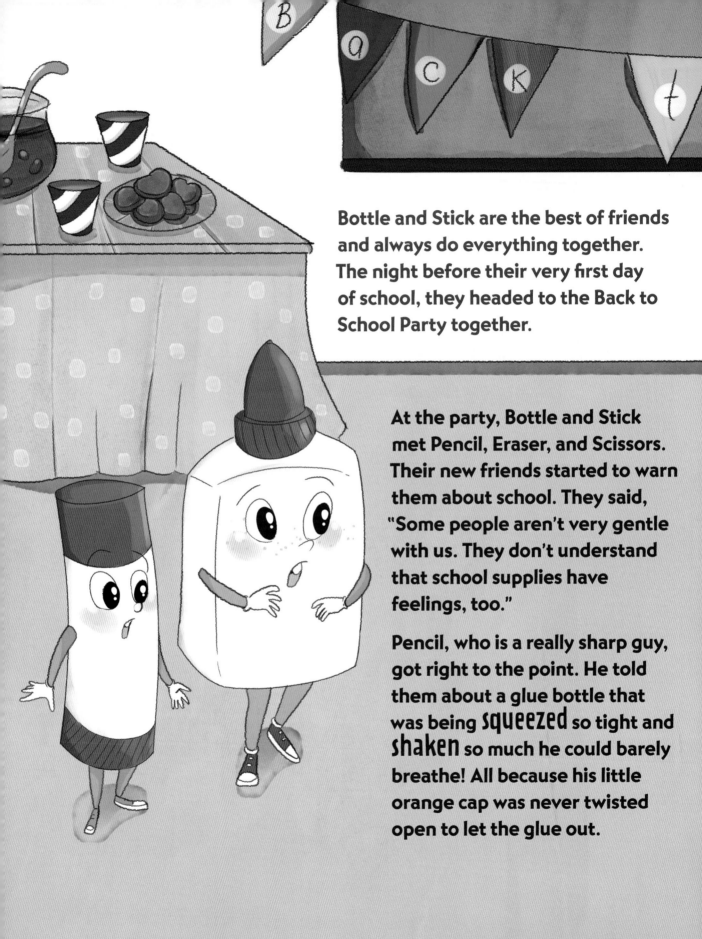

Bottle and Stick are the best of friends and always do everything together. The night before their very first day of school, they headed to the Back to School Party together.

At the party, Bottle and Stick met Pencil, Eraser, and Scissors. Their new friends started to warn them about school. They said, "Some people aren't very gentle with us. They don't understand that school supplies have feelings, too."

Pencil, who is a really sharp guy, got right to the point. He told them about a glue bottle that was being squeezed so tight and shaken so much he could barely breathe! All because his little orange cap was never twisted open to let the glue out.

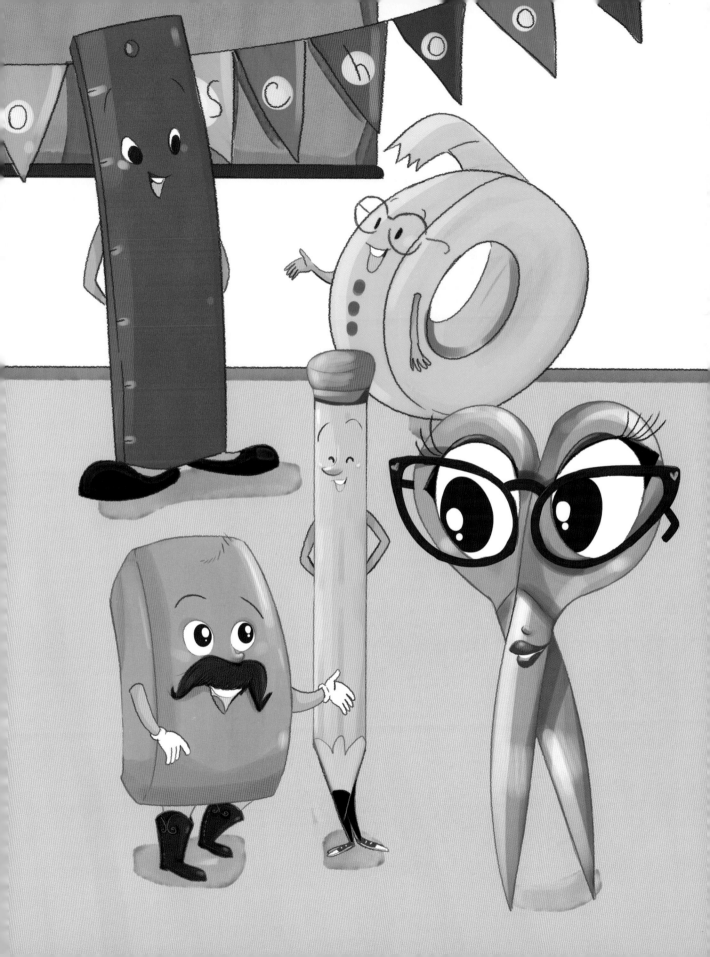

Bottle touched his own little cap and gulped, thinking maybe school wasn't the place for him.

Stick felt bad for Bottle, but was secretly relieved to be wearing a rigid, plastic suit of armor.

Pencil noticed the look of relief on Stick's face and said, "You don't have to worry about squeezes, Stick, but you *do* have to watch out for dizzy spells!"

Pencil told Stick about the time a glue stick was twisted and twisted and twisted up as high as it would go, instead of being turned just a teeny bit. Before Stick could respond, Eraser joined them.

Eraser, who is known for fixing mistakes, told
them about the trouble with glue lids.
"Lids!" exclaimed Eraser, shaking his head.
"Bottle lids left open.
Stick lids falling to the floor and rolling away.
It's *sooo* frustrating to see my friends just...dry up.
I can't even fix it, and I fix *everything*!"

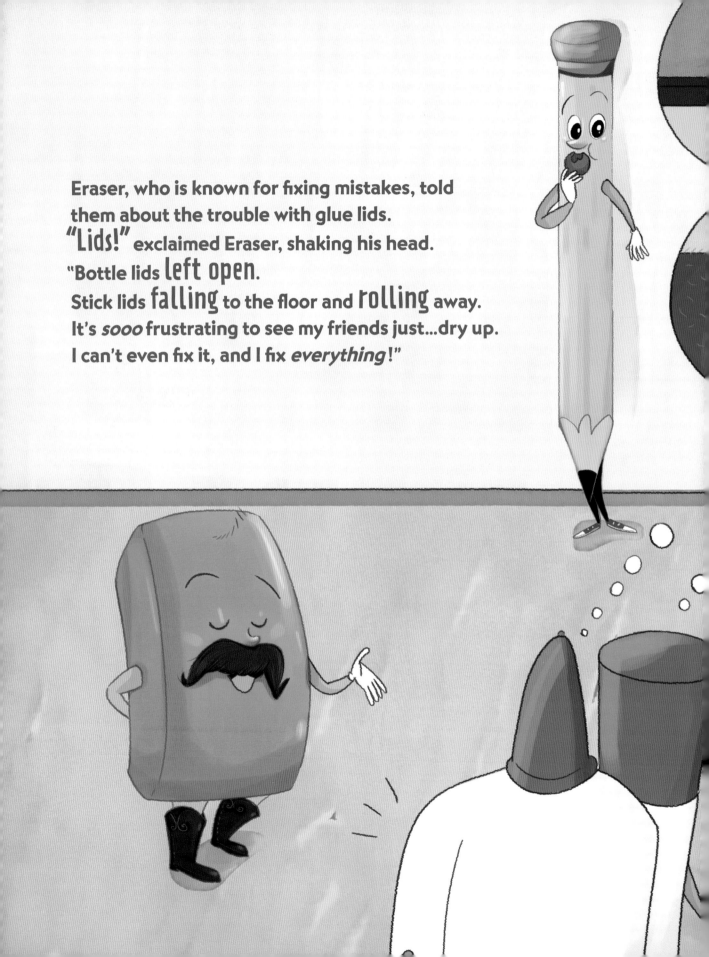

Bottle and Stick were standing there with their mouths wide open in disbelief when Scissors cut in. She told them about the biggest problem of all...too much glue! Scissors said, "Bottles get SQUEEZED until globs and globs of glue get everywhere! And sticks are SMOOShed all over into a giant, globby, purple-y MESS!"

Finally, it was time to go. Bottle and Stick said good-bye to their new friends. On the way home, they considered everything Pencil, Eraser, and Scissors warned them about...

They didn't want to be squeezed, twisted, dried up, or wasted.

At home, Bottle got busy packing their lunches. Stick went online to make sure they had the right bus number.

They both picked out their special first-day outfits. Then, it was time for bed. They climbed into their comfy bunk beds, closed their eyes, and were soon fast asleep.

The next morning, Bottle, who's usually the brave one, was feeling nervous about going to school! He even started to cry. Bottle said, "I'm just not sure if...school is right for me. Pencil, Eraser, and Scissors make school seem so...so...*scary.*"

Stick, feeling more confident than Bottle, said, "I think if we just remember to stick together, we can do anything! We might even really like school."

"Do you really think so?" asked Bottle wearily.

"YES!" exclaimed Stick. Bottle hoped Stick was right.

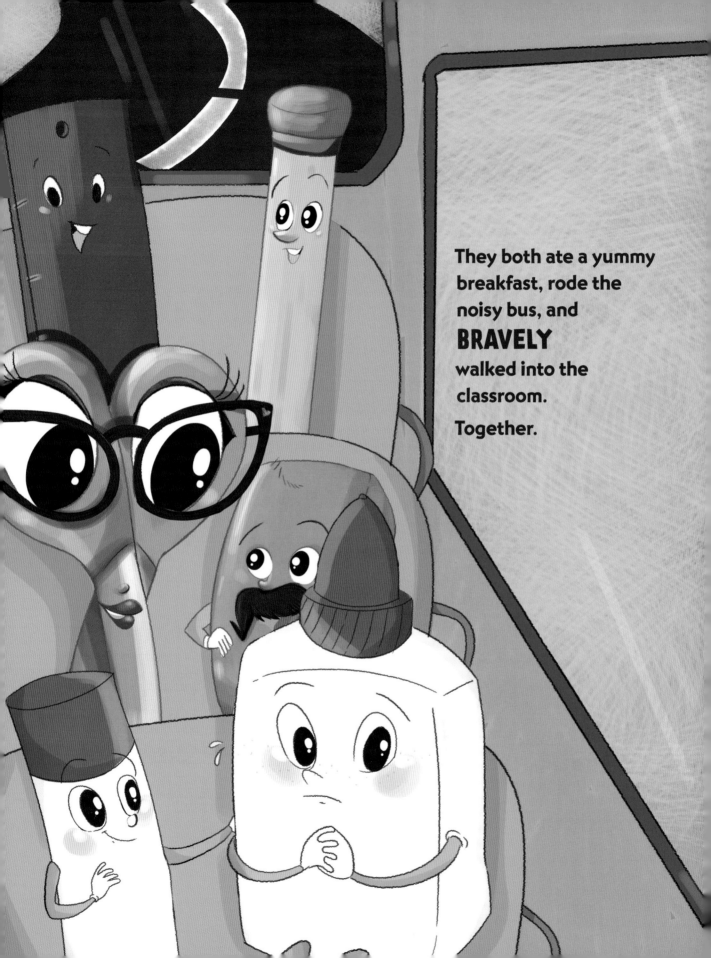

They both ate a yummy breakfast, rode the noisy bus, and **BRAVELY** walked into the classroom.

Together.

And after just a few mishaps, everybody learned the glue rules and were very responsible with Bottle and Stick. Everyone at school took care of Bottle and Stick, always remembered to put their lids back on, and weren't ever wasteful with them. Bottle and Stick had a **MARVELOUS** time! Sticking together, of course.

Gentle!

Lids don't get lost or left open.

Use one dot!

Extra glue? Wipe it off!

The End

Jennifer Stephens

is a first grade teacher and, now, an author! Jennifer has spent nearly thirty years in the classroom tirelessly picking up hundreds of lost glue lids, wiping down glue-covered desks, and teaching kids that we are braver when we stick together. She earned a Master of Arts in Teaching from Webster University and served as Teacher of the Year for her school in 2011. She lives in Lees Summit, Missouri, with her husband and two fearless Chihuahuas.

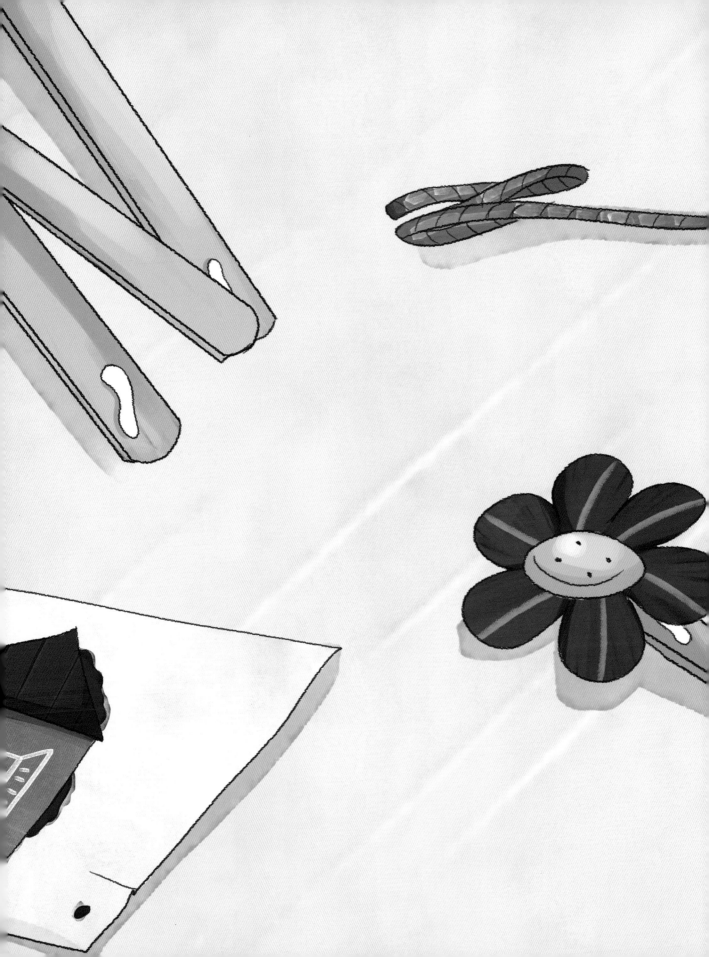

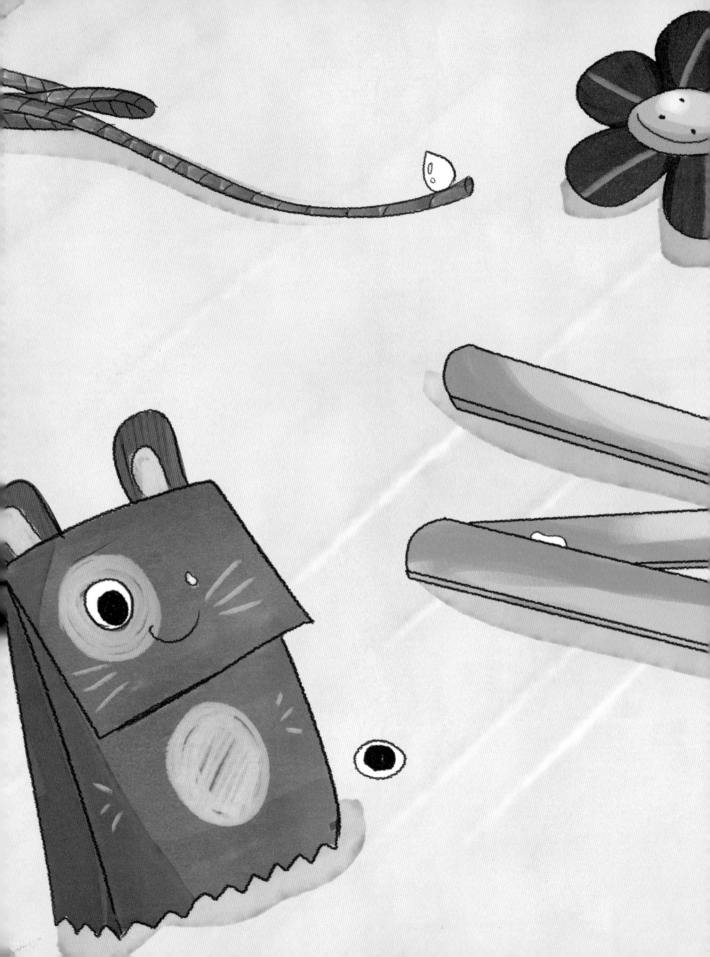